For Alfie Bloom - DP

For Tilly - NP

Text copyright © 2009
by Daniel Postgate
Illustrations copyright ©
2009 by Nick Price

All rights reserved. Published by
Chicken House, an imprint of Scholastic
Inc., *Publishers since 1920.*
Published in the United Kingdom by
Chicken House, 2 Palmer Street, Frome,
Somerset BA11 1DS. www.doublecluck.com
CHICKEN HOUSE, SCHOLASTIC, and associated
logos are trademarks and/or registered trademarks
of Scholastic Inc. www.scholastic.com

Library of Congress Cataloging-in-Publication Data
Postgate, Daniel. • The snagglegrollop / Daniel Postgate ; illustrated by Nick Price. • p. cm. • Summary: Sam and his parents discover
that the imaginary creature he has made up is a wonderful pet which can do amazing things, including giving Sam courage to
speak to a classmate he would like to have as a friend. • ISBN-13: 978-0-545-10470-8 • ISBN-10: 0-545-10470-X • [1. Imaginary
creatures—Fiction. 2. Pets—Fiction. 3. Friendship—Fiction. 4. Family life—Fiction.] I. Price, Nick (Nicholas R.), ill. II. Title.
PZ7.P8387Snc 2009 • [E] —dc22
                       2008033784

10 9 8 7 6 5 4 3 2 1   09 10 11 12 13

Printed in Singapore • First American edition, May 2009
Body text was set in Chaloops Regular. Display text was set in Chaloops Bold. Book design by Susan Schultz

The SNAGGLE GROLLOP

By Daniel Postgate

Illustrated by Nick Price

Chicken House

Scholastic Inc. / New York

"Can I have a **dog?**" asked Sam.
"**No,**" said his dad. "I'll have to take it for walks all the time."

"Can I have a **cat?**" asked Sam.

"**No,**" said his mom. "They leave fur all over the furniture."

"How about a **snagglegrollop**, can I have one of **them?**" asked Sam.

"What's a **snagglegrollop?**" asked Mom.

"I don't know," said Sam. "I just made it up."

His parents laughed.
"Well . . . if you just made
it up, then, **yes,** you can have a
snagglegrollop!" said Dad.

After school, Sam came home with a **strange**-looking creature.
"What on earth is **that?**" exclaimed Dad.

"It's a **snagglegrollop**," said Sam.
"You said I could have one, remember?"

"Yes, but . . . no, but . . . but — **oh golly**," spluttered Dad.
"Well, it's **your** responsibility. You are the one who
has to look after it."

The **snagglegrollop** took quite a lot of looking after.

It was very **hairy**, so it took a long time to wash . . .

. . . and dry.

It was very big,
so it needed **huge**
amounts of food.

And it had very big teeth,
so it used all the tubes of toothpaste.

But it told **hilarious** jokes, and was a **superb** dancer,

and on weekends it
took the family out on
fabulous adventures.

They soon became very fond of
their **snagglegrollop.**

But sometimes the **snagglegrollop** seemed
rather **sad**. At night it would sit out on
the roof of the garden shed and
stare at the **stars**.

One day at school, Emily Evans

(who Sam liked a lot but was too afraid to speak to)

said that her parents wouldn't let her have a cat.

"You could ask for a **snagglegrollop**," said Sam bravely.

"What's **that?**" asked Emily.

"I don't know," said Sam. "I just made it up."

Emily laughed. "I think I would prefer to
have a **quibblesnuff!**" she said.

Sam, Dad, and the **snagglegrollop** were playing **hide-and-seek** in the park one afternoon when Emily arrived with her **quibblesnuff**.

Sam's snagglegrollop was enchanted.

They told each other **hilarious** jokes . . .

. . . and they danced together
superbly.

Then, hand in hand, they flew up into the sky

They flew once around the park, waved good-bye, and flew off into the distance.

"I didn't know they could do **that**," said Sam. "Do you think we'll ever see them again?"

"I don't know," said Emily. "Perhaps it doesn't matter, as long as they're **happy**."

"Can Emily come back to our house after school one day?" Sam asked his dad.

"Of course she can," said Dad.

"And can I have a **dog**?" asked Sam.

"Maybe," said his dad. "We'll see."